# TOO MANY TRIBBLES!

By Frank Berrios

Based on the original teleplay "The Trouble with Tribbles"
written by David Gerrold

Illustrated by Ethen Beavers

A GOLDEN BOOK • NEW YORK

TM & © 2019 CBS Studios Inc. STAR TREK and related marks and logos are trademarks of CBS Studios Inc. All Rights Reserved. Published in the United States by Golden Books, an imprint of Random House Children's Books, a division of Penguin Random House LLC, 1745 Broadway, New York, NY 10019, and in Canada by Penguin Random House Canada Limited, Toronto. Golden Books, A Golden Book, A Little Golden Book, the G colophon, and the distinctive gold spine are registered trademarks of Penguin Random House LLC.

rhcbooks.com

ISBN 978-1-9848-4800-0 (trade) — ISBN 978-1-9848-4801-7 (ebook)

Printed in the United States of America

10 9 8 7 6 5 4 3 2 1

## CAPTAIN'S LOG, STARDATE 4523.3.

Captain Kirk and the crew of the U.S.S. *Enterprise* have received an urgent call from Deep Space Station K7. Could it be a Klingon attack?

Upon arrival, Kirk and Mr. Spock learn their true mission from an assistant named Darvin: they must protect a shipment of high-yield grain. The greedy Klingons will probably try to steal it for themselves!

While two guards keep the grain secure, the rest of the crew explores the station. Lieutenant Uhura meets a trader who sells furry little creatures called tribbles.

The salesman gives Uhura a tribble as a gift.
Uhura loves her new furry pet!

Uhura returns to the *Enterprise* with her hungry little tribble. The next morning, she is shocked to discover that she has a *bunch* of new tribbles!

Suddenly, a Klingon battle cruiser arrives
at the space station. This could mean trouble!

The Klingons are allowed to board the space station . . . but can they be trusted? Not even furry little tribbles like Klingons!

Although the Klingons say they come in peace, a fight breaks out! No one insults the *Enterprise* in front of Scotty!

Meanwhile, back on the *Enterprise*, the bridge is covered in tribbles!

The tribbles got into the air vents, so they are now all over the ship—even in the mess hall! And they're eating everything in sight!

If the tribbles were able to find their way into the air vents aboard the _Enterprise_, they must have done the same on the space station!

Captain Kirk and Mr. Spock beam back aboard the space station . . .

. . . and their fears are confirmed! The tribbles have eaten all the grain!

Mr. Spock notices that some of the tribbles
are sick. Someone must have poisoned the grain!

With a little help from Dr. McCoy and a couple of tribbles, Kirk discovers that Darvin is a Klingon spy in disguise! Darvin was the one who poisoned the grain.

With their spy revealed, the Klingons quickly leave the space station. The crew returns to the *Enterprise*—but all the tribbles are gone!

Where did all the tribbles go? It turns out that Scotty transported the furry creatures to the Klingon ship, where they'll be no *tribble* at all!